Building Wings

How I Made It Through School

by
Don Johnston

with Jerry Stemach

Don Johnston Incorporated
Volo, Illinois

Edited by:

Jerry Stemach, MS, CCC-SLP

Gail Portnuff Venable, MS, CCC-SLP

Dorothy Tyack, MA

Consultant:

Ted S. Hasselbring, PhD

Graphics and Illustrations:

Photographs and illustrations are all created professionally and modified to provide the best possible support for the intended reader.

Pages 69: NASA

All other photos © Don Johnston Incorporated and its licensors.

Narration:

Professional actors and actresses read the text to build excitement and to model research-based elements of fluency: intonation, stress, prosody, phrase groupings and rate.

The rate has been set to maximize comprehension for the reader.

Published by:

Don Johnston Incorporated
26799 West Commerce Drive
Volo, IL 60073

800.999.4660 USA Canada
800.889.5242 Technical Support
www.donjohnston.com

DON JOHNSTON

International Standard Book Number
ISBN: 978-1-4105-0782-2

Contents

Chapter 1

Welcome to My World

This is the company I started. It's called Don Johnston Incorporated.

Hello, my name is Don Johnston and for many years, teachers told me I had a learning problem. And for most of my life, I believed there was nothing I could do about it.

Some of my classmates called me stupid. Some of my teachers said I was lazy. But then I found out something that changed my life. I found out that I *could* learn — I just learned in a different way. I also found out that there are many other students who learn in different ways — just like me.

I found out that it is *my* job to figure out how I learn. It is *my* job, not my teachers' job, to take charge of my learning.

Teachers may tell you that *you* have a learning problem. What they really mean is that you don't learn like most other students. You need to figure out how you *do* learn. And then you need to make sure it happens. Teachers can help you, but they can't make you successful. You have to do that for yourself. My story will show you how I became successful. You can do it, too.

I am 55 years old, but don't think of me as some old guy who can't feel your pain or know what you're going through. By the end of this book, you'll see that I've been there, done that, and still struggle today. But guess what? I got through it. I figured it out.

Today I am married to a wonderful person, Cheryll, and we have two wonderful boys, Ben and Kevin. I started my own business making books like this for students who struggle. After Ben and Kevin finished college, they came to work in my company.

This is my family at my son Kevin's graduation. Kevin is on the left and next to him is me and then my older son Ben. My wife Cheryll is standing in the front.

But I was 14 years old before I could read my first book from cover-to-cover.

I'm sure you know how it feels to have people look at you as if you are stupid. You also know how it feels to struggle and even fail in school. You're not alone. People called *me* stupid, lazy, and a troublemaker.

But I wasn't stupid back then, and I'm not stupid now. I wasn't lazy back then, and I'm not lazy now. OK. So I *was* a troublemaker. But that's how I got out of looking stupid. It worked for me.

You and I are smart and
hard-working people *if* we are given
something that we understand and *if* we
are *interested* in doing it. We may be
different from other students, but we
can be successful too.

Sometimes students say to me,
"You're successful, but what about me?
Can *I* be successful with a learning
problem?" You can be successful if
you want to. But I'll be honest and tell
you it's going to be hard work. You will
have to work harder than other people.
You will have to learn about yourself.
You will have to find out *how* you learn.

You know what? A big part of the reason that I'm successful is because I learn differently. That means I *think* differently, too. I have overcome bigger problems than most people. I have worked harder than most people and I learned to keep going even when I felt like a complete failure.

I have solved many of my own problems, and you will have to solve many of your own problems. But you can be successful, just like me. If *I* tell you that, you should believe it, because I still struggle with learning, but I don't let my struggle bring me down.

So let's go on a journey together. I'll tell you what happened to me. My stories may sound different from your stories, but I bet they are really the same stories in many ways. I discovered how I learn, and you will need to discover how you learn. Don't expect to wake up one morning and understand yourself completely. It will take time. But don't get down on yourself. Whenever I get down on myself, I stop learning.

Chapter 2

I Start School

This is me when I was five years old.

I want to tell you my story about growing up and struggling in school to learn. For me, it's a painful story — so painful that I didn't even talk about it until I was about 40 years old. And when I *did* start telling this story, I woke up in the middle of the night all sweaty and afraid because I remembered some awful things that had happened to me as a student. What kinds of awful things? Keep reading.

This is the house where I grew up. When I was five years old, I used to sit on the front steps and watch the kids from my neighborhood come home from school. They were carrying books and laughing. Meanwhile, I was stuck at home with nothing to do. I'd ask my mother, "When do I get to go to school?"

"Sooner than you think," she said. It felt more like forever to me.

I can remember sitting at a desk at home trying to write. I couldn't make the shapes of some of the letters, but I sure worked at it.

This is the house where I grew up. That's my mother and
my dog outside the house.

I had no idea how to read words in a book, so I just looked at the pictures. *That's OK*, I thought. *I'll learn to read and write when I start school. School will be fun.*

I don't remember much about starting kindergarten, but I do remember that my mother drove me to school. Other new students were crying. Not me. I just wanted to run into the classroom and get started with learning.

When Mom and I walked into the class, there were square tables with four chairs around each table. These were our "desks." The teacher pointed to a chair near her and told me to sit down. I ran to the chair, sat down, and waved good-bye to my mom. My mom looked kind of sad.

I thought, *OK, I'm ready to start school NOW*. I rocked from side to side in my chair. I picked at a spot on the table with my fingernail. My legs were moving. "When do we start?" I asked out loud. I wanted school NOW!

One day, our teacher told us to sit on the floor and make something with the pile of blocks that she had put there. I really got into it. I decided to make a really tall building.

After a while, the teacher told us to stop and go back to our desks. I didn't hear her. I kept stacking my blocks higher and higher. The other students returned to their desks, so I took their blocks and kept making my building higher.

It's the best building in the class, I thought. I was almost finished when the teacher yelled at me, "Don, return to your desk!" I turned and saw that I was the only student still on the floor.

"But I'm not done," I said.

The teacher was angry. "Return to your desk right now!" she said.

I stood up and walked slowly to my desk. I looked over at my building. I wanted to finish it. I really liked it. It was much bigger than the other buildings.

Doesn't she see what a good job I did? I wondered. I looked at the teacher and tried to figure out why she was so upset with me. *I made a great building. Why doesn't she like it? Why doesn't she like* me?

In kindergarten, I never could please my teacher. Maybe first grade would be better.

Chapter 3

What's Wrong with Me?

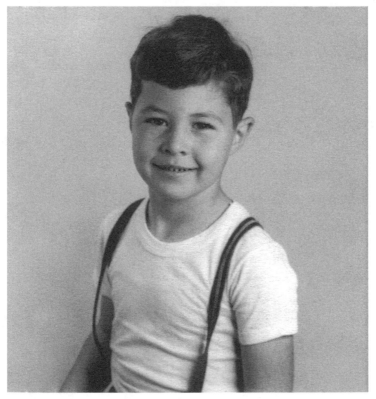

A photo of me in first grade

On the first day of first grade, my teacher, Mrs. Arns, passed out books, paper, and pencils. Then she said, "By the end of first grade, you will be able to write a letter to a friend."

Wow! That's cool. I'm going to work really hard this year and be a great student, I promised myself.

My promise only lasted one day. On the second day, Mrs. Arns stood in front of the class, then looked at me and said, "Don, I've heard that *you* are a troublemaker, but you won't be a troublemaker in *my* class."

Me?   A troublemaker?   I thought about what Mrs. Arns said.   Had she been talking to my kindergarten teacher? *I* didn't think I was a troublemaker.

First grade was hard.   I did learn some of the letters of the alphabet, but many letters just wouldn't stick in my brain.   I would learn a letter and then — *BAM!* — five minutes later, it was gone. It seemed like Mrs. Arns only asked me the letters that I didn't know, and she always got mad when I couldn't give the right answer.

Mrs. Arns would say, "Don, pay attention."

But I am paying attention, I thought. I felt stupid that I couldn't remember the stupid letters of the stupid alphabet, so I dreamed about being a great baseball player.

One day, Mrs. Arns wrote the letters H – O – W on the board. Then she called on me. "Don, what is this word?'" I stared at the word. I had no idea. "Pay attention, Don," Mrs. Arns yelled. "You are *so* lazy."

I looked around at the class. The other students were laughing at me. *Thanks a lot, Mrs. Arns,* I thought. *Now the whole class thinks I'm stupid and lazy.* I smiled at them, but inside I was thinking, *What's wrong with me?* From that day on, I went to school with an upset stomach because I was afraid of failing.

As soon as the bell rang to go home, my stomach stopped hurting. I was off to play baseball on the street in front of my house.

The kind of baseball we played was called "soaky." The ball was made out of old socks. When a "soaky" ball is dry, it's soft. You don't need a glove to catch it, and you can't break a window.

But sometimes we played in the rain and the ball got completely soaked. Now the "soaky" would really fly when you hit it. Now it was hard. It was hard enough to break a window. And we did break a few windows.

We played ball until it was too dark to see. We laughed and we had a great time, and I never thought about school until the next morning.

Mrs. Arns had divided the class into three reading groups. Of course, I was in Group Three, the group that had the most trouble in reading. I liked Group Three, because we didn't have to read in front of the class, and the other kids in my group didn't laugh at me.

After a few weeks, Mrs. Arns moved two students out of Group Three and up into Group Two. They were happy. She also moved two students out of Group Two and down into my group. They were sad. One of those kids was a pretty girl with blond hair named Marilyn. She cried because the class thought that any kid in Group Three was a failure for sure.

I liked Marilyn. She never laughed at me like the other students did. I wished I knew what to say to make her feel better. I smiled at her and she smiled back. Then, a few weeks later, she was gone! Just like that, she was back in Group Two. I was happy for her, but I missed her. I thought we could never be friends because she would think I was too stupid.

The other kids in Group Three seemed to be doing better than me and one other boy named Jimmy Lucas.

I wondered if Jimmy and I would ever catch up. I took my reading book home and tried reading to my mother. She would repeat a word that I missed, but the next time I saw the word, I forgot it again. The words were not sticking in my head.

One day my grandmother came to visit. She had been a teacher, so my mom wanted me to read to her. Grandma was sure that *she* could fix my problem. She would smile and teach me a word, but five minutes later — *BAM!* — it was gone from my head.

Now Grandma looked worried. I was scared. What was wrong with me? I wasn't going to be writing a letter to a friend any time soon.

Chapter 4

The Worst Moment in My Life

Mrs. Arns stood in front of the class and said, "Starting today, there will be four groups for reading. I'm going to call the new group the Baby Reading Group."

I could feel a pain in my stomach and in my chest. It was hard to breathe.

Mrs. Arns said, "Jimmy and Don are the Baby Readers. They can't read what the rest of the class is reading, so they will start over with the reading book that we used at the beginning of the year."

The rest of the class laughed. I could feel my eyes fill up with tears and a kind of lump in my throat. I thought, *Don't cry. Don't cry. Don't show anyone how you feel inside.* I stared at the blackboard. I held my breath, then swallowed hard to hold back the tears.

Mrs. Arns called Jimmy and me to the back of the room. I was trying so hard to hide my feelings that I didn't hear her.

Mrs. Arns said, "Don, you're not paying attention *again*. I said come back here. This is why you are in the Baby Reading Group. You just don't pay attention."

As I walked to the back of the room, everyone was looking at me. I looked at the floor. I tried to smile but I just couldn't.

Mrs. Arns handed us our book. *The class is way past this book*, I thought.

When I started to read, I whispered the words so none of the kids could hear me. "See Puff run. Funny, funny Puff." Puff was a cat, and she was old news to the rest of the class. Many of the students turned around and looked at Jimmy and me. They were smiling and looking at each other.

"The rest of you can turn around and get back to work, or you will be in the Baby Reading Group, too," said Mrs. Arns.

By the time reading group was over, my body was shaking. I just stared at my desk for the rest of the day. But I did learn something on that day. I learned that I could hold my breath as a way of keeping my feelings from exploding.

Maybe I'm stupid but at least I can play baseball, I thought. *Maybe I can be a baseball player when I grow up.*

Slowly, I was learning to read some easy words, words like *how, run, did, up.*

But everyone else was learning much faster than me. Well, maybe everyone except Jimmy. But the other kids were reading really hard words — words that I couldn't even begin to read. Would I ever catch up? I didn't think so.

I couldn't wait for the school year to be over. I didn't like Mrs. Arns and she didn't like me. I counted the days until summer vacation. As I walked home on the last day of school I was so happy.

My friends and I were singing, "School's out, school's out, teacher let the bulls out. No more pencils, no more books, no more teacher's dirty looks."

I got dirty looks *every day* from Mrs. Arns. It had been an awful year. Next year *had* to be better. At least I was finished with Mrs. Arns. Or so I thought.

Chapter 5

Hiding It from Jack

A photo of me in second grade

Summer vacation was over and it was time to go back to school. I didn't want to go back to school. My older brother was sure that this year would be better. He was right. My new teacher was Mrs. Crowshore, and I liked her right away. She was a kind and gentle woman who hardly ever got angry.

In first grade, I never talked to my friends at school. In second grade, things were a little more relaxed. For one thing, Mrs. Crowshore didn't have a Baby Reading Group.

I was still in the group with the worst readers, but two friends from my neighborhood were also in that group. Their names were Dana and Raymond. They were poor students, too, but they were a few steps ahead of me.

I hated reading in front of the class. One day, Mrs. Crowshore asked me to stand up and read. The sentence in the book started out like this, *The world is big and . . .* But I had no idea how to read the word *world*.

I tried to read it. "The wo . . . the wor . . . ral . . ." I began.

The other kids started to laugh. Mrs. Crowshore said to them, "It's not nice to laugh at others. You don't know every word, either."

I felt safe in her class, but I did not look forward to the walk home from school. There were about six of us who lived in the same part of town, and it took us about 20 minutes to get there. Jack — the bully — was always making fun of someone.

That day Jack turned to the others and said, "Can you believe that Don didn't know how to read the word *world* today?" He looked at me and said, "You're such an idiot." Then he laughed his bully laugh and yelled, "You are sooooo stupid."

The other kids laughed along with him, because that's what you did around a bully like Jack.

"OK, Don," said Jack. "What word is this? H-o-u-s-e."

I had no idea. Everyone laughed again.

"Try this," said Jack. He spelled out the word table. "T-a-b-l-e."

It sounded like a bunch of letters to me. I said, "Spell it again." Everyone laughed *again*.

When I got home, I went to my bedroom, shut the door, and cried. After about 30 minutes, Dana and Raymond came by to play baseball.

"I don't feel like it," I said.

"Don't worry about Jack," said Raymond. "Jack makes fun of all of us."

"Yes, but he doesn't call you *stupid*," I said.

"He calls us plenty of other names," said Dana. "Come out and play baseball. We need you. We play the team on Main Street next week. We have to get ready."

"OK, I'll be right out," I said. Once again, I was saved by baseball.

For the next several years, there was no way that I could read books at my grade level. Books at my grade level were way too hard to read. When I was about ten, I decided to try reading books that were really easy. I walked downtown to the public library, then I waited for all the kids my age to leave. I didn't want them to see what I was about to do.

First, I got two books that *were* at my grade level even though I couldn't read them.

Then I went to the part of the library where they keep books for little kids. Most of these books have lots of pictures in them. In fact, they are called picture books. They also have sentences that are easy to read.

If I looked at the pictures in these books carefully, I could usually figure out all the hard words in the sentences. I knew that Jack would really let me have it if he knew that I was reading picture books, so I hid them between the two hard books. It worked! And it was helping me to become a better reader.

But one day, when I was walking to school with the kids from my neighborhood, someone bumped into me and my books went flying. Jack took one look at the picture books and said, "Look! Don reads baby books." Everyone laughed. Then Jack started in on me, "You are so lame, Don. How could anyone be so stupid?" More laughing.

I picked up my books and walked away. I could hear them laughing for a long time.

For the next few months, I walked to school by myself. I stopped reading picture books, too, even though they had been helping me learn how to read.

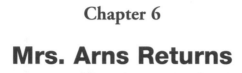

Chapter 6

Mrs. Arns Returns

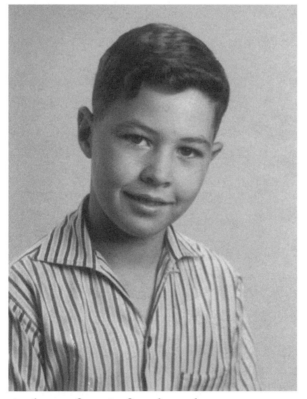

A photo of me in fourth grade

There's nothing worse than having other kids laugh at you because you can't read or write. By the time I started fourth grade, I was very good at covering up my learning problems. In some ways, I was making progress with my learning, but I knew I was still far behind the other students.

When I walked into the fourth-grade classroom at the beginning of the year, I was shocked to see my first-grade teacher, Mrs. Arns, standing at the front of the room. *She's my teacher?* I thought. *Oh, no!*

First grade was a bad dream, but three years had passed since I first met Mrs. Arns. Maybe *she* wasn't any different, but *I* was. I had become an expert troublemaker.

Mrs. Arns started with me by saying, "You are a troublemaker just like your brother."

It was one thing to call *me* a troublemaker in front of the other students, but calling my *brother* a troublemaker was too much. This was all-out war.

The more Mrs. Arns tried to embarrass me, the more I tried to get into trouble. The more I got into trouble, the more she embarrassed me. I didn't care any more. That year, I wasn't in class very much. I spent most of my time in the corner, in the hallway, or in the principal's office.

By the end of fourth grade, I was even farther behind the other students. I didn't learn anything about reading, writing, history, or math that year. But I was learning a few tricks that got me out of reading in front of the class.

I learned that you should never look the teacher in the eye while she is picking the next person to read. I also learned that you should never look like you're bored. If you look bored, the teacher will always call on you because teachers — even a bad teacher like Mrs. Arns — think that no one could ever be bored in *their* classes.

Some teachers go down each row and make every student take a turn at reading. I usually found a way to get in trouble right before it was my turn.

I would do anything to avoid reading in front of the class. Sometimes, I would start coughing until the teacher asked me if I needed a drink of water. I would nod my head "yes" and go out to the drinking fountain until my turn to read had passed.

Sometimes I might fake an emergency and say that I needed to go to the bathroom. If nothing else worked, I would stand up to read, then fall over onto another student. That always worked. I usually got sent to the principal's office for that one.

I didn't like going to the principal's office, but it sure was better than having kids laugh at me because I couldn't read.

I never said to myself, *Gee, I think I'll have a behavior problem so I won't have to read.* No. When it got close to my turn to read, I started to panic. I had to do something — anything — to get out of reading. I knew that other kids would think I was stupid as soon as they heard me try to read. Besides, other students *enjoyed* seeing me get into trouble. They never saw my behavior as a cover-up for my learning problems.

A good joke worked sometimes. If a kid called me dumb or stupid, I might say, "Well, I'm smarter than Jimmy Lucas." I don't know if I *was* smarter than Jimmy, but my joke got a laugh and it saved me from looking bad in front of others.

Oh, and Mrs. Arns? She retired after her second year of teaching me.

Chapter 7

Spaced Out

This is a photo of my father.

One day when I was about seven years old, my dad came home from work and turned on the television to watch the news. He usually didn't watch the news until late at night, so I knew that something important must have happened that day. I sat down and watched the news with him.

The man on TV said that Russia — also called the Soviet Union — had sent a satellite into outer space. The satellite was now traveling in circles around Earth. The scientists in Russia had named their satellite *Sputnik*.

Sputnik

I asked my dad why he was so interested in a Russian spaceship. It didn't have any people on board, so what harm could it do?

"Russia wants to be the most powerful country in the world," said my dad. "But America thinks that *it* is the most powerful country. The people of America think that we are smarter than the Russians, but now the Russians have won the race into outer space. So maybe their scientists *are* better than our scientists."

"Are you worried about this, Dad?" I asked.

"Well, they say that with a satellite like *Sputnik*, Russia could attack us from outer space with a nuclear bomb," Dad said.

I had heard about nuclear bombs. A nuclear bomb is the most powerful kind of bomb in the world. At the end of World War II, the United States dropped nuclear bombs on cities in Japan and killed hundreds of thousands of people.

If the Soviet Union decided to drop a nuclear bomb on the United States from outer space, there was nothing that we could do to stop them.

A few months after *Sputnik*, Russia sent up another satellite. Meanwhile, the scientists in the United States were still planning their first space flight.

I started going out into my backyard at night and looking up at the sky.

Many times I saw those Russian satellites in the sky at night. They looked like tiny stars moving across the darkness. I thought a lot about how satellites could be used to destroy the world, or how they could be used to discover other places in space. I spent hours wondering if there was life on other planets. *If there* is *life on other planets, what do those creatures look like?* I asked myself. *Do they live in houses? Do they drive cars or spaceships? Do they go to work and school like we do?*

I needed more information because now I was really, really interested in knowing about rockets and spaceships and outer space. But the information I needed was in books, and I couldn't read. That's about the time that I met Rudy.

Chapter 8

Rudy to the Rescue

I had never talked with anyone about my interest in space until I started hanging out with Rudy. He had the same questions as I did.

"I wonder how long it would take for a spaceship to reach Earth from another planet?" Rudy asked.

"How far away *are* the planets?" I asked. "How about the stars? How much farther away are the stars?"

Rudy and I would stop at his house after school and look at his books about space.

Then we would go to my house and look at my books. Rudy wasn't a good reader either, so we needed pictures to help us answer these questions.

Here are some things we learned. Russia sent a man into space in April 1961. Then, in May, the United States sent a man named Alan Shepard into space, and the "space race" was on! John Kennedy was president of the United States back then, and he made an announcement that the United States would send a man to the moon in less than ten years!

"Wow, Rudy, this is exciting stuff," I said. Rudy and I wanted even more information about the race to the moon. After school, we were off looking for information about space, the moon, rockets, and astronauts. We tried to read the newspaper, but we could only look at the pictures and guess what the story was about.

We watched the news on TV every night. Then, we'd meet up the next day and talk about what we had learned.

"Hey Rudy, did you see the news?" I asked.

"What's going on?" he asked.

"In about a week, the United States is going to send John Glenn into space. He's going to circle the earth three times and then splash down in the Atlantic Ocean. They say he will be traveling about 17,000 miles an hour. How fast is that, Rudy?" I asked.

"Well," said Rudy, "how fast can a race car go?"

"I don't know," I said. "We better go look that up."

Chapter 9

We Make a Rocket

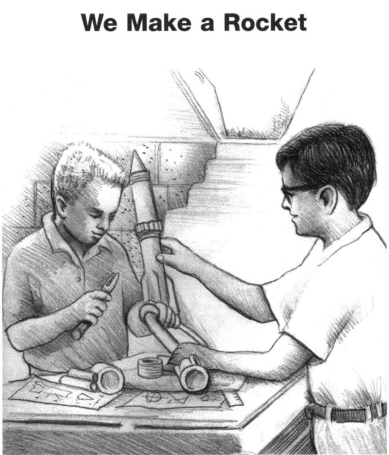

Rudy's house had a great basement. A basement is a room under a house. In most houses, you can go down into the basement from inside the house. At Rudy's house, you had to go outside, then back in through the basement door.

Rudy's mom hardly ever went down in the basement, so she never checked up on us. That was good because we were building rockets down there.

It's easy to build something that *looks* like a rocket, but it's not so easy to make it fly. You need something that will push or "propel" the rocket into the air.

Scientists spend a lot of time thinking about this problem of making a good propellant. A propellant is a strong force that pushes in one direction and moves you in the opposite direction. Air inside a balloon becomes a propellant when you let go of the balloon and all the air rushes out, sending the balloon flying around the room.

Rudy and I were trying to find a good, strong propellant for our rockets. At first we used balloons. We would build a rocket out of cardboard and paper.

Then, Rudy and I would stuff a balloon into the rocket and fill the balloon with air. But we could never get the rocket to take off correctly, so our rockets crashed soon after take-off. We did discover that long balloons worked better than small, round ones, and a small, light rocket flew better than a large, heavy one. These discoveries were not exactly rocket science.

That's when we decided to make a *real* propellant.

Rudy and I each had a chemistry set. We mixed different chemicals together, then we tried to light the chemicals on fire. Sometimes we added things that we found in Rudy's garage. Some things worked but most things didn't. It's amazing that we didn't blow up Rudy's basement, or set ourselves on fire. Sometimes we made a lot of noise down there, but Rudy's mom never seemed to hear a thing.

Back in those days, when the scientists launched their rockets into space, they always showed it on TV. I don't think I ever missed a launch. I would get up around 4 or 5 o'clock in the morning, tip-toe into the living room, and turn on the television. I sat right next to the TV on the floor so I could hear. Sometimes, my mom would wake up.

"Don, go back to bed," my mom would say. "You have school this morning."

"In a minute," I'd say. "They're ready to launch."

One time my dad got up and watched a launch with me. He asked me questions, and I answered them. He looked surprised that I knew so much about the space program. I told him all about the mission and what the scientists wanted to learn. Then I told him about the next two missions.

From then on, my dad always asked me to report on the space program at the dinner table.

Wow, I knew more about the space program than *he* did.

Chapter 10

Mrs. Tedesco Believes in Me

A photo of me in eighth grade

I often wonder what my life would be like today if Mrs. Tedesco had not been my teacher in eighth grade. Would I have become a good student without her? Would I have become successful? Maybe, but I don't think so. Mrs. Tedesco *believed* in me, and every student needs someone like that.

"You have Mrs. Tedesco?" the other kids said. "She is so hard. You won't get away with anything."

Great, I thought. *I'm in for another bad year*.

Right away, Mrs. Tedesco said, "Don, I want to see you after class."

Now what? I thought.

"Don, I expect you to do well in my class this year," she said.

I didn't know what to say. "OK," I told her. I never had a teacher talk to me like this before.

Just wait until she talks to my other teachers, I thought. *She will give up on me, too, just like they did. This year won't be any different.*

After a few more days, Mrs. Tedesco said, "Don, I want to see you after class." This time she told me that she was unhappy with my work.

"Don, I expect more from you," she said.

"I've never been a good student," I said. "I'm probably the worst student in your class." I had never admitted this out loud, and I was surprised that I had said it. My learning problems had always been *my* secret.

"Don, you have the *potential* to be a good student, but you are not working up to your potential," Mrs. Tedesco said. "I expect you to do much better. I expect you to work hard this year. I'm putting your homework at the top of my pile so I will look at it first every night."

Yikes!

She looked at me as though she could see right into my brain. I was scared.

Then Mrs. Tedesco said something that
I still hear to this day:

*"Don, you can do it. I know
you can."*

She was completely confident that I
could do it.

She was completely confident,
but I was completely confused. Was
she crazy? Was this a trick she was
using to control my behavior? That's
all my other teachers had wanted:
good behavior.

But Mrs. Tedesco didn't seem to be worried about my behavior. She wanted me to be successful. She was *demanding* that I be successful.

One day the class was discussing how people first came to North America thousands of years ago. Mrs. Tedesco asked a question, and I raised my hand and answered it. Then I asked, "Why would people want to leave their homes and go to a new place they didn't know? If they came here by boat, where did they get tools to build the boats?"

Mrs. Tedesco told me what she knew. Then she said that there was still a lot that wasn't known about this topic. She turned to me and said, "Don, *nice thought*."

For one short moment, everything in the world stopped. *Nice thought?* This was the first time in eight years of school that any teacher had ever given me a compliment. I looked around the class to see if the other students were laughing at me. They were *not* laughing. They wanted to know the answers to my questions, too.

That's all it took for me.   One simple compliment.   No upset stomach. Heck, I wasn't even trying hard.   *Maybe, I* can *do this,* I thought.   Now I really started paying attention in class.   Now I really did study hard, and every night I spent hours on my homework.

Chapter 11

The Movies in My Mind

Smart kids know a lot of facts, so I tried to memorize facts. But memorizing facts was hard for me. If there were five facts to remember about the Roman Empire, I could only remember two facts. One day, I wrote down a bunch of facts, then I asked my mom and dad to ask me a question about the facts. It was no good. I just couldn't get those facts to stick in my head. The next day, Mrs. Tedesco wanted to see me again after class.

"Don, I don't need you to tell me the facts that we are learning," Mrs Tedesco said. "I want to know what you *think* about the facts. I want you to give me your opinion about the facts. Can you do that?"

"I'm not sure that I understand what you mean," I said.

"Do you remember when you asked me questions in class the other day?" she said. "Those were really good questions. You have to be a good thinker to ask good questions. Learning is about thinking."

Then a strange thing happened. The more I started *thinking* about what we were studying, the easier it was to remember the facts. Facts began to stick in my head — and I didn't even have to try to make it happen.

Here's how I would think about things. I would look at a picture in a book and think about it until I could make the picture change into a movie that I could watch inside my head.

If we were studying about the Roman army in England, I would look at a picture of a battle. Then I would see the people in the picture start to move until it felt like I was watching a movie. I might see the general of the Roman army riding his horse and telling his soldiers to charge the enemy. I might think, *why doesn't he wait a little longer before they charge?* This really got me thinking about the battle and the war. The more thinking I did, the easier it was for me to learn.

OK, maybe it wasn't perfect. I still had trouble remembering important dates and the names of important people, but I was thinking now and asking questions, and I was really learning.

All my other teachers had only called on me when they were pretty sure that I *didn't* know the answer. Mrs. Tedesco called on me when I *did* know the answer. She didn't ask me for facts. She asked me for my *opinion*. She had respect for me and I had respect for her.

I started to feel like a good person and a good student. I discovered that I even *enjoyed* school and learning. I was becoming confident. Maybe I wasn't an A student, but I was getting C's and that was a giant step up from D's and F's.

After my eighth-grade year, I never thanked Mrs. Tedesco for what she had done for me. But I did thank her 35 years later. I found out where she lived and one afternoon, I went to visit her.

This is my teacher Mrs. Tedesco today.

"Mrs. Tedesco," I said to her. "You made me believe in myself. You were truly interested in my opinion. You showed me that I could learn and become a successful student. My life is different because of you. Thanks."

Chapter 12

The Puzzle

Baseball saved my life.

I started ninth grade in a new school where we got to choose our classes. I chose a math class — Algebra — but the school said "no" because I had gotten mostly D's in math all through grade school and middle school.

"But I want to take Algebra," I said. "I *need* to take Algebra."

After a lot of talking back and forth, the school agreed to let me take Algebra.

Algebra was easy for me. I started getting C's, then B's, then A's.

I had never gotten a B or an A in any class in my life. Kids in my class used to laugh at me, but they weren't laughing now. Now they were asking me to help them with their Algebra homework.

Even Jack — remember Jack, the bully? — even Jack came up to me and said, "So, Don, do you know how to do problem five?"

"Yes, Jack," I said, "but there's a trick to it." I showed him the trick, but he still didn't get it. He just stared at me.

"Tell me how to do it step-by-step," Jack said.

"Step-by-step?" I said. "I don't use steps when I solve a math problem. I make pictures in my head."

Jack didn't laugh at me when I said this, and he never made fun of me again.

Suddenly many students were asking me for help with Algebra — the same students who had laughed at me in grade school.

One of these students said to me, "Don, what happened to you?"

"What do you mean?" I asked.

"How did you become so smart?" he wanted to know.

Then I thought, *If I can get good grades in Algebra, why can't I learn to read?*

I was interested in space and in people who invent things, so I bought a book called *Breakthroughs in Science*.

The book was full of stories about famous inventors who had made great discoveries. The book had more words than pictures, but I decided to give it a try.

The way that I had been reading so far wasn't working, so I decided to try something new. Mrs. Tedesco had taught me that learning was about thinking. When I thought, I put pictures in my head and sometimes I turned the pictures into movies. Maybe this could work for reading, too.

In the past, I would try to read each word by sounding out each letter. If I couldn't read a word, I kept trying until I could. But I read so slowly that I never understood what I read. If I did read fast enough to understand, I couldn't remember what I read.

When I read *Breakthroughs in Science*, I turned the words into pictures and a movie. If I didn't know a word, I made a guess at it and kept on reading. It worked!

In ninth grade, *Breakthroughs in Science* was the first chapter book I ever read *and understood* from beginning to end. Mrs. Tedesco had taught me that learning was about thinking. *Reading is also about thinking*, I thought. For me, thinking and reading meant putting pictures and movies in my head.

I started looking for other books about things that I was interested in. I gave each book the picture and movie test. If I couldn't make pictures or a movie out of the words, I picked another book.

Pretty soon I was reading a book a week. Wow. I had become a reader at last.

Reading textbooks at school was a different story. Textbooks were just too hard. They were full of dates and facts, and I couldn't turn that kind of information into pictures. My classmates knew all the words in these books because they had been reading for eight years. They had much more information than I did.

Try to imagine a creature from outer space landing on earth and starting school in ninth grade. If the creature had never heard words like *Rome, England, Canada*, or the *United States*, it would have a hard time learning about history. In ninth grade, I was just like a creature dropping in from outer space.

For me, learning about a subject like the Roman Empire was like starting a brand new jigsaw puzzle.

My classmates had started learning about the Roman Empire in fifth grade, so they had already put a lot of the pieces to this puzzle together. My pieces were still in the box.

For example, my classmates already knew that Rome was a city in Italy and that Italy was a country in Europe. They knew that the Roman Empire stretched from England to Egypt. What did I know? I knew that Roman soldiers wore shiny helmets and fought in battles, because I had seen a picture like that in a book long ago.

Chapter 13

Success at Last

Here's me in my football uniform in ninth grade.

Even though the textbooks were hard, I began to be successful at doing homework for the first time. In grade school, my parents had needed to *force* me to do homework. Now when they came into my room, they saw books open everywhere.

One day my dad asked me why I needed to have so many books open at the same time.

"Well," I said, "we're studying about the Middle Ages in Europe."

"That book on my pillow has maps of the world in it." I said. "I didn't know where England was so I looked in that book. The book on the floor is open to a map of France."

"What about those books?" asked Dad, pointing to the books on my desk.

"Check this out, Dad. This book shows pictures of soldiers wearing suits of armor. Can you imagine what it was like to wear something as heavy as that? And look at this book. It shows a horse wearing a suit of armor, too.

How could a man or a horse ever run in stuff like that?"

"And those three books on your bed?" my dad asked.

"I'm doing a book report for English class," I said. "I'm choosing the book I want to write about."

My dad left the room looking worried.

A little while later, my mom came in and said, "Don, are you having trouble with your friends at school again?"

"What do you mean?" I asked.

"Well," said my mom, "you spend all of your time studying and I don't see you spending any time with your friends. You don't even watch TV any more."

"TV is pretty boring," I said. "And I *do* hang out with my friends after school. But after dinner, I really need to study. I need to catch up to the other kids. They are way ahead of me in school."

I met a new friend at my new school named Al Joe. We played football together.

Here I am, batting in Pony League.

Then, when baseball season rolled around, Al Joe asked me to be on his team in Pony League. Pony League is the next league after Junior League, so it's for older players.

Our team ended up going all the way to the finals and playing in the championship game for Western Pennsylvania. We played in front of a very large crowd. The game was close, and I made a diving catch that stopped two runs from scoring. We won the championship by one run.

After that, Al Joe and I had a lot of fun together. We liked to go to the next town and try to meet girls. We were always going somewhere and doing things together.

There was something special about Al Joe. He was really funny. He always had his friends and his teachers laughing. He also happened to be the smartest kid in the school. When it was time to study, Al Joe studied. He really liked to have fun, but when it was time to do his homework, Al Joe said "no" to fun and "yes" to work.

One day Al Joe asked me to study for a test with him. I didn't know what to expect. For me, studying meant sticking my nose in a book or in my notes. For Al Joe, studying meant spending a few minutes looking over his notes. He would write his notes on cards. Each note had its own card. After he had studied a note on one of the cards, he would put the card away. Then Al Joe and I would talk about that note. It was just like talking about the weather. It wasn't as hard as trying to memorize facts.

After a while, I looked at my watch and said, "OK, when are we going to start *studying*?"

Al Joe said, "What do you mean? We *are* studying."

"Just talking about this stuff isn't studying," I said.

"Oh, yes it is," said Al Joe. "Talking about what we learn is really important. You'll see tomorrow when we take the test. Talking will help you remember."

Al Joe was right. We both did well on the test. After that, I started to talk with my mom and dad at dinner about what I was learning in school. I was eating dinner *and* I was studying.

I had a lot to learn to make up for what I had missed. I worked really hard and it paid off. By the end of ninth grade, I was getting A's in Algebra and B's and C's in my other subjects. By the end of high school, I was getting A's and B's in all my classes. Success at last.

Here I am with my date for the junior prom.

I had become a good enough student to think about going to college. I knew now that if I worked hard, I could do anything I wanted.

Maybe I'll study about students who have learning problems. Maybe I'll start a school for those students. Maybe I'll learn how to use a camera and become a photographer. Maybe I'll travel all over the world. Maybe I'll start a business. Maybe I'll fly my own airplane. It won't be easy, but I can do it! I thought to myself.

This is my graduation from high school.

Guess what? I *did* do all those things, and no, it wasn't easy. But it was worth it, and I'm still learning new things every day.

You can too. I know you can do it.

The End

About the Start-to-Finish Author and Narrator

Don Johnston started a company in 1980 to help students become better learners. He started this company because he struggled with learning.

Don's company makes books and software to help all students be successful.

Don is a photographer, and he enjoys traveling around the world to take pictures. Some of the pictures that you will see in Start-to-Finish books were taken by Don.

About the Start-to-Finish Author

Jerry Stemach is a writer and teacher who has lived in northern California all of his life. His home now is in the Valley of the Moon. This valley is famous for wine, and Jerry and his wife, Beverly, grow grapes on their land. They have two daughters, Sarah and Kristie.

Jerry has helped struggling readers for over 30 years. He is the author of the *Nick Ford Mysteries*. Before he writes a mystery, he travels to where the mystery will take place to take photos and to talk with the people who live there.